MR. YOWDER AND THE
LION ROAR CAPSULES

Library of Congress Cataloging in Publication Data

Rounds, Glen, 1906–
   Mr. Yowder and the lion roar capsules.

   SUMMARY: Finding that the old lion he is given in
trade is totally useless except for his roar,
Mr. Yowder attempts to capitalize on that one asset.
   [1. Humorous stories]   I. Title.
PZ7.R761Mi   [Fic]   75-35607
ISBN 0-8234-0272-X

Weekly Reader Children's Book Club Edition

Weekly Reader Children's Book Club presents

MR. YOWDER AND THE LION ROAR CAPSULES

written and illustrated by GLEN ROUNDS

Holiday House, New York

At the time I speak of Mr. Xenon Zebulon Yowder, the sign painter, was living just outside Lee's Summit (or Peculiar, or Gunn City or some such place) in Missouri.

This was in the time of what was later called The Great Depression—a time when almost nobody had any money to speak of—and a great many had even less than that. So, not having money to spend, people had gotten into the way of trading things they had but could get along without for things they needed more. This was known as Taking in Trade, or Barter.

Even in hard times such as those, people in business had to have a certain number of signs painted, and Mr. Yowder managed to stay right busy. Sometimes he was paid in cash for his work, but mostly he simply took whatever useful items a customer offered instead. What he couldn't use himself could eventually be traded off to someone else. But in the meantime finding a place to store these things came to be something of a problem.

When he'd first come to town Mr. Yowder had rented a nice room from the Widow Lucas. The Widow was an understanding woman, and she said nothing the day she was sweeping out his room and found he'd stacked six bushel baskets of apples and a bag of Bermuda onions in the corner beside his bureau. Nor did she say anything later when she found a crate of eggs, an old set of buggy harness and six cedar posts stored under his bed. She knew that in times like those a man had to take whatever he could get in return for his work, and so far Mr. Yowder had always managed to take in enough cash to pay his room rent each week.

But even so, she was a neat housekeeper, and there was a limit to her under-standing. And that limit was reached the day she found six Rhode Island Red hens and a young tom turkey shut in his closet, and a big gray goose walking around the room hissing at her when she tried to sweep. That evening she told Mr. Yowder he had to move.

Mr. Yowder agreed that the room *was* getting just a mite cluttered, perhaps. And, furthermore, that very day he'd taken in four Pekin Ducks and a small goat in payment for a sign he'd painted over in Raytown.

So he loaded his things into the back of his old car, said good-bye to the Widow Lucas and moved out to an abandoned farm just past the edge of town. Nobody was using it at the time and he had plenty of room to store his growing collection of things taken in trade.

As I say, in spite of the Great Depression Mr. Yowder was doing right well. Around the barber shops, filling stations and feedstores men told one another that there was nothing, no matter how unlikely, that Mr. Yowder wouldn't take in trade for painting a sign. And always, they said, he'd somehow manage to make at least a small profit on the deal.

Almost everybody agreed that, one way or another, Mr. Yowder would one day be a very rich man.

Then came the day . . . when the owner of a small traveling circus offered to trade him a lion for some fancy lettering on his circus wagons.

"A real live lion?" Mr. Yowder asked him.

"Yessir!" the circus man said. "That one right over there," and he pointed out a small beat-up cage on wheels over on the back of the lot.

Now if that had been a cow, a horse, a shoat or some other familiar form of livestock he'd been offered, Mr. Yowder would have examined it very carefully before agreeing to the trade. For it is a well-known fact that such creatures vary widely in value, depending on their age, general health and the condition of their joints, teeth and other parts.

But lions, to the average person, are something special—like Santa Claus, the Government, or the President; mention "lion" to anybody you know (if he's not already in the lion business) and the chances are his eyes will glaze over as he thinks of brass bands, clowns, ladies in pink tights standing tippy-toe on galloping white horses and things like that.

And Mr. Yowder, in that respect, was no different from anybody else—shrewd trader though he was. He was so taken with the idea of being the only sign painter in Missouri—and maybe in the whole United States—to own a real live lion that it never occurred to him to suspect that the creature might not really be the bargain he seemed to be.

So . . . before the man could change his mind Mr. Yowder shook hands on the deal and hurried off to collect his lion. When he'd finally gotten the cage hooked behind his car, he waved good-bye to the circus man and drove off the lot—without doubt the happiest sign painter in the whole state of Missouri.

As Mr. Yowder knew it would, the story of the sign painter who hauled a lion around in a cage hooked behind his car did spread around the state. But somehow or other the results weren't quite what he'd expected.

The truth was, the lion was unbelievably old and scarred-up. His eyes were bleary and filmed over and most of his yellowed teeth were worn down or broken off, and some skin ailment had laid bare great patches of his hide. His joints were swollen by arthritis or rheumatism or some such trouble so that he walked and moved with great difficulty; and in addition to these things, probably due to his great age, ailments and slovenly habits, he smelled terrible.

All in all, he was anything but an attractive beast. And Mr. Yowder soon learned that instead of crowding around the cage, as he'd expected, people tended to hold their noses and hurry past—on the upwind side if possible. And children who got too close to the cage were dragged away by their mothers before they caught something dreadful from that "awful animal!"

People wanting signs painted soon began to ask Mr. Yowder to please not bring the old lion with him, or if he did to park the cage around the corner somewhere out of sight. And worse yet, the word began to spread among the loafers in the barber shops and around the filling stations that Mr. Yowder had at last met his match—that he'd been outtraded by a circus man.

By now he was beginning to worry. Not only was the lion making him the laughingstock of the country, he was also eating him out of house and home. Like most folk who have never had any dealings with lions, it had never occurred to him to wonder how much it took to feed one. If he had thought about it at all, he'd probably have supposed that, like his hounds, the animal would be satisfied with table scraps and maybe a beef bone now and again.

But he quickly discovered that his table scraps, even with extra hush puppies thrown in, were only appetizers for that old lion. Some days he ate a half dozen chickens, a turkey or two and maybe a rabbit—and still licked his feed pan hungrily. At the rate Mr. Yowder's supply of livestock was disappearing, he would soon have to begin to think about buying lion feed, which would be expensive as well as difficult to find.

So he began to rack his brain trying to figure some way to get rid of the lion, and if possible to make at least a small profit at the same time. Surely the creature, old as he was, should be good for something.

He advertised LION FOR SALE, CHEAP in both the *Kansas City Star* and *The Grit,* but there didn't seem to be much demand for secondhand lions that year. And it was obvious that the hide wasn't worth lifting, since there wasn't hair enough on it to make a rug.

The only healthy thing about that animal was his roar. When he wasn't eating or sleeping—and being right old he didn't sleep much—he roared. On those swollen arthritic feet he'd shuffle up to one end of the cage and stand looking out over the neighborhood. Then he'd start pulling himself together. He'd strain until he'd slowly raised his tail to the level of his back, brace himself, take a deep breath, lay back his ears and ROAR. After that he'd drop his tail, stand a moment seeming to be listening to what he'd done, then slowly, and with considerable difficulty, he'd turn around in that narrow cage and get ready to roar again in the other direction.

Day in and day out, night and day, that lion roared on the average of three times an hour, and over a few weeks that adds up to a lot of lion roars.

Up to now, selling lion roars was the only thing Mr. Yowder hadn't considered. But here he was with a lion that was really nothing but a live lion roar factory, so the best thing to do was to try to figure out a way to sell lion roars.

But when he thought about it he realized that there were surprisingly few people in ordinary life who had any real interest in either lions or lion roars. Circuses, however, were another matter—there were dozens of them scattered over the country, and nearly all of them owned from six to forty lions.

As nearly as he could figure the biggest reason for having lions in the circus was so that their roaring in the menagerie tent just before show time would draw the crowds to the ticket wagons. Of course ticket selling is a very

LIVE LION   STUFFED LION

important part of the circus business, but Mr. Yowder knew from experience how much it cost to feed just one lion. So when he thought about what it was costing those circuses to feed theirs, he figured they were paying a terribly high price for their lion roars, even if they were buying their meat wholesale. It stood to reason that if somebody came along and showed them how they could get their lion roars cheaper they'd be glad to talk business.

So now all Mr. Yowder had to do was figure out a way to preserve lion roars for later use. If he could do that the circuses could replace their expensive live lions with stuffed ones (a first class stuffed lion in those days cost only ten or twelve dollars) and save a great deal of money. Then whenever they wanted to draw a crowd all they'd have to do would be to open a can or two of lion roars, and let them out among the cages with the stuffed lions in them.

For several days he spent all his time studying and measuring lion roars as the old lion roared them. He found that a lion roar was usually about four feet seven or eight inches long, and about as big around as his arm. Also, he found, it was about ninety-nine percent air.

Now Mr. Yowder knew that it was possible to compress a great deal of air into a very small space, so it was logical to suppose that the same thing could be done with lion roars. But the problem was to find something to put them in once they were compressed.

He thought about that for several days. Then one day he was in the back of Doc Overton's drugstore watching him put up some malaria medicine, scooping the bitter quinine into one half of a gelatine capsule, then slipping the other half on to cap it. And that was when Mr. Yowder got his idea. If he could put each compressed lion roar into its own capsule, all the circus people would have to do when they wanted lion roars would be to throw a handful into a bucket of water. In a few minutes the capsules would dissolve and out would come the lion roars as good as new.

So he bought a box of empty capsules, the biggest Doc had, on credit, and hurried home to try the idea out. On the way he stopped and borrowed an old air compressor that stood behind the filling station and set it up in front of the lion's cage. After putting an old gramophone horn on the front for the lion to roar into, he started the machine up.

The compressor was a small one, and when the first lion roar started through it the machine banged and rocked, then choked down altogether. Mr. Yowder hadn't realized a lion roar was so tough. So he went back downtown to hunt up a bigger compressor, and it was nearly sundown by the time he got back and the new machine set up. But this time things worked better, and the lion roars went through the compressor without trouble.

But a lion roar, even when compressed, is a little hard to see and at first Mr. Yowder had trouble telling what was lion roar and what was just plain compressed air. However, with practice his judgment improved and he finally caught one and stuffed it into a capsule before it got away. That was the world's very first Lion Roar Capsule!

All the rest of the afternoon Mr. Yowder compressed lion roars as fast as the old lion roared them. At first he had trouble stuffing a compressed roar into its capsule without breaking parts of it off, but by the end of the afternoon he had a half dozen Lion Roar Capsules that looked to be almost perfect.

However, he knew that even the best thought-out ideas can go wrong, so he decided to try a few of these capsules out, just to be sure they worked.

Stuffing the little box of Lion Roars in his pocket, he started to walk to town. On the way he passed the yard of a lady who had a number of cats she thought right highly of. They were gathered around a big dish of warm milk she'd just put out, so Mr. Yowder leaned over the fence and dropped a Lion Roar Capsule into the dish. For a minute or two nothing happened and the cats went on lapping up the milk.

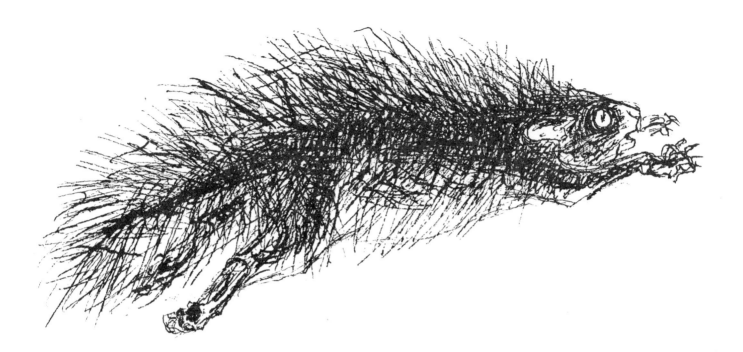

Then the capsule, softened by the milk, suddenly came apart and let the lion roar loose right in the faces of those startled cats! In spite of having been run through an air compressor and then jammed into that small capsule, it was still as fine a lion roar as any one would care to hear.

Mr. Yowder was vastly pleased by this proof that his idea would work, but what the cats thought was another matter. They simply took off in whatever direction they happened to be facing and left that place. A big Persian, finding his way blocked by the sycamore, turned neither to the right nor to the left but climbed straight up to the very topmost twig.

Mr. Yowder also left the neighborhood without delay, and downtown he turned into the alley behind the feed store. The back room was a sort of club for the town checkers players, and while he didn't play checkers himself, he thought it might be a good place to give his Lion Roar Capsules one more tryout.

As he'd expected there were already four men gathered around the old table in a clear space between the stacks of feed and fertilizer. Judge Hapgood and Filthy Bill, the town barber, were playing while a farmer named Rabbit Box Johnson and a drummer from the hotel held down the spectators' chairs. Mr. Yowder said howdy all around and sat down on a bag of oats to watch the game.

Judge Hapgood raised hunting dogs in his spare time and this night he had a fine setter pup lying beside his chair. Later, while the Judge was concentrating on the problem of how to avoid Filthy Bill's move to corner his king, Mr. Yowder reached out and took the pup in his lap. He petted him a while, then slipped a Lion Roar Capsule well back in his mouth, rubbed his throat until he'd swallowed it and put him back on the floor beside the Judge's chair.

A few moments later, while all four men at the table were concentrating on the Judge's problem, the pup hiccuped as pups are in the habit of doing. But instead of being an ordinary hiccup this one was a full-sized lion roar. Coming as it did from under the table and echoing back and forth from the walls of that small room, it was truly a fearsome sound—especially to men not familiar with lion roars.

Like the cats earlier in the evening, the checkers players left that place and were across the high loading platform and some yards up the alley before they even tried to disentangle themselves from the table legs and the chairs.

The pup followed them by shortcuts he knew through backyards, and was home scratching on the door by the time the Judge got there. He wasn't hurt, but somehow or other he never did amount to much as a hunting dog—he couldn't stand loud noises of any kind.

Mr. Yowder walked home slowly, dreaming of being rich. He knew now that all he had to do when the circus came to Kansas City in a couple of weeks was go to see the circus men and let them watch while he dropped a handful of Real Roaring Lion Roar Capsules into a bucket of water. When they heard those real lion roars boiling up out of the water as the capsules dissolved, and heard his plan of replacing the expensive live lions with cheap stuffed ones, he'd be in business. Mr. Yowder knew that when fellows like that saw a way to save money they didn't hesitate to take advantage of it. That's how they got rich enough to go into the circus business in the first place.

After that Mr. Yowder stopped painting signs entirely and spent all his time compressing lion roars. So by the time Circus Day came he had about seventy dozen Lion Roar Capsules put away in the cellar where it was cool. He didn't know if they'd spoil, but he was taking no chances.

He'd had a printer print up some handsome gummed labels that said YOWDER'S REAL ROARING LION ROAR CAPSULES in red letters. And Doc Overton had sold him some little cardboard boxes with partitions inside to keep the capsules from rattling around. Each box held thirty-six compressed lion roars, and Mr. Yowder figured the circus people would be glad to pay at least fifty cents a roar.

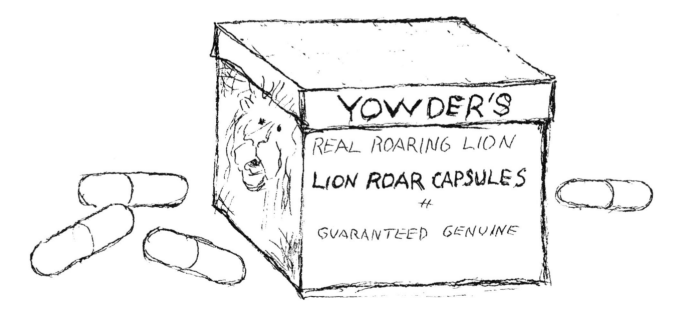

Right after breakfast on Circus Day he fed the old lion, carried the boxes of lion roars out of the cellar and loaded them into the back of his old car. What with one thing and another all these chores had taken a good deal of time, and so it was after noon before he finally got onto the road.

As he drove along he thought about the stories that would be told around over the country about how he had made a fortune out of the beat-up old lion nobody else wanted. Now and again he heard a little thunder behind him, but the sun was shining where he was so he didn't pay it much mind.

It was just before he came to the bridge across the Little Blue River, about where the Raytown Road turns off, that somebody's old hound trotted out onto the road ahead and stopped, looking the other way.

To avoid hitting the hound Mr. Yowder stepped hard on the brakes, and by the time he'd stopped he found himself soaked to the skin by heavy rain. Looking around he found the back of the car full of water to the tops of the doors and the lion roar boxes afloat.

What had happened was that for some time he'd been driving just in the front edge of one of the small but violent rainstorms that are common in that country. Until he'd slowed for the hound, rain had been falling steadily into the backseat, but none into the front. Such things can happen in Missouri.

Mr. Yowder tried to save some of the floating boxes but the cardboard was already soaked, and the capsules themselves were beginning to soften. While he watched, the first lion roar came bubbling up from among the sodden boxes and roared off across Jackson County. It was closely followed by another, and in what seemed to Mr. Yowder to be only seconds his lion roars were streaking away in all directions. There was nothing he could do but hold his hands over his ears and let them go.

It is a well-established fact that a lion roar can be heard for about a mile and a half on a quiet day, so it is reasonable to suppose that several end to end could be heard much farther. And here were lion roars going out in strings of a dozen or more in any direction you wanted to listen, so there is no telling just how far away that uproar was heard.

Horses ran away with farmers in the fields, windows shattered, dogs and chickens went under the houses and refused to come out for days after. Even old Granny North, who hadn't heard a word anyone said to her for over forty years, claimed she'd heard lion roars roaring by her house in Lone Jack that day. It was told later that down towards Knob Noster the sky turned black as night and a great wind came up. It could have been so, but stories do tend to grow in the telling after any such catastrophe. However, it was generally agreed that there hadn't been such excitement in that part of the country since Quantrill's last raid, back in Jayhawker days.

When the last of his lion roars had finally gone out of hearing, Mr. Yowder sat for a while waiting for the ringing to leave his ears. Then he got out, cranked up his car and turned back for home.

This was a terrible setback to his plans for going into the lion roar business, but he figured he still had his lion and he should be able to replace the lost lion roars in time to meet the circus again when it showed in Jefferson City later in the summer.

However, it turned out that his troubles were still not over.

When he drove into the yard, the first thing he noticed was that the lion's cage was empty. Looking closer he found that the rotten floorboards had finally given way beneath the old lion's weight, and he'd fallen out through the bottom. Nowhere was he to be seen. Mr. Yowder was still searching the sheds and hen houses when he heard the train whistle.

Looking across the little pasture he saw the old lion standing on the railroad embankment beyond. Somehow, old and crippled with rheumatism as he was, and half-blind besides, that feeble old creature had managed to get through the wire fence and up the steep embankment, and now stood braced squarely between the rails, facing the oncoming train!

It was a fast freight with two locomotives, and while the whistles screamed and sparks flew from the brake shoes and sliding wheels, the old lion began to pull himself together. He slowly raised his head, stiffened his tail straight out behind him, opened his mouth wide and finally ROARED right in the oncoming locomotive's face!

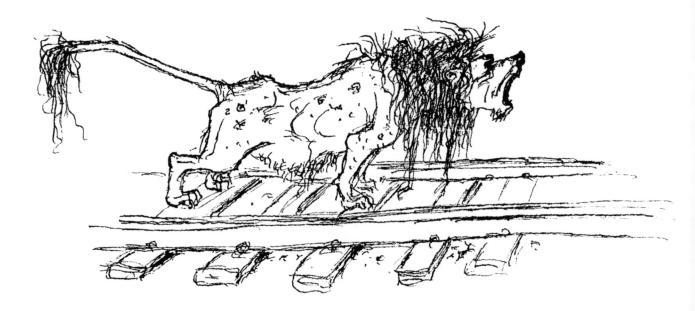

The train didn't stop and for a while there was nothing to be seen through the clouds of steam, dust and coal smoke. Then, after the last of the hundred and seventy-two cars and the caboose had passed, Mr. Yowder slowly climbed the bank and looked about.

But there was nothing left of the lion except for a few scattered bits and pieces, and a few tufts of coarse tawny hair caught on nearby bushes.

Mr. Yowder carefully gathered up all the bits he could find and buried them in a small grave beside the right of way.

Later he traded a sign for a small white monument with TO THE MEMORY OF A BRAVE LION carved onto it and set it up to mark the spot. It can still be seen, if you look close, a few feet to the right of milepost 623 beside the tracks of the Kansas, Topeka and Santa Fe.

Losing the lion put Mr. Yowder out of the lion roar business, of course. As far as anyone knows he gave up all hopes of ever being rich, and probably is still painting signs somewhere in Missouri, or Kansas, or Oklahoma or some such place.